The U

The Utterly Nutty History of Footy
The Utterly Nutty World of Sport
The Utterly Nutty World of Animals
The Utterly Nutty World of the Future

Martin Chatterton was born in Liverpool in 1961. He has been an illustrator, designer and author since 1983 and has illustrated over seventy children's books and written twelve more in joined up writing all by himself.

He lives in Southport and is married with two children, Sophie and Danny, plays centre-forward for Birkdale Rovers and is currently in Los Angeles where he is discussing a six picture, multi-figure motion picture deal with MetroGlobalMonster Studios. His first movie, Nutty Footy: Now the Screaming Starts, starring Leonardo DiCaprio as Michael Owen, and Cameron Diaz as Dwight Yorke, will begin shooting later this year . . .

Editor's note: the publishers would like to point out that they have absolutely no control over the author's appearance and would like to reassure those of a nervous disposition that Martin Chatterton is kept under strict twenty-four hour supervision in an exclusive Beverly Hills Rest Home.

PUFFIN BOOKS

Published by the Penguin Group
Penguin Books Ltd, 27 Wrights Lane, London W8 5TZ, England
Penguin Putnam Inc., 375 Hudson Street, New York, New York 10014, USA
Penguin Books Australia Ltd, Ringwood, Victoria, Australia
Penguin Books Canada Ltd, 10 Alcorn Avenue, Toronto, Ontario, Canada M4V 3B2
Penguin Books (NZ) Ltd, Private Bag 102902, NSMC, Auckland, New Zealand

On the World Wide Web at: www.penguin.com

Penguin Books Ltd, Registered Offices: Harmondsworth, Middlesex, England

First published 1999
1 3 5 7 9 10 8 6 4 2

Made and printed in England by Clays Ltd, St Ives plc

British Library Cataloguing in Publication Data
A CIP catalogue record for this book is available from the British Library

ISBN 0–141–30447–2

The Utterly Nutty World of The Movies!

Written and illustrated by
Martin Chatterton

PUFFIN BOOKS

CONTENTS

How to Make Your Very Own Nutty Blockbuster!

If you've ever dreamed of being the next Steven Spielberg or James Cameron (they're film directors, doofus!) but don't know your tracking dolly from your pan fade, your jump cut from your final edit, we're here to help.

Just follow Channel Nutty's step-by-step guide to creating your very own celluloid masterpiece and before you can say 'Action!' you'll be flogging it to Hollywood for major spondoolicks!*

Before you can buy that yacht in the South of France, the ski lodge at Aspen and the private Lear jet, there are one or two essential items you will need to get off the ground and into the wonderful world of moviemaking . . .

Ingredient 1. The Sunglasses

You need to get a decent pair of sunglasses if you want to make any sort of an impresssion as a Hollywood director. Obviously it would make your image more convincing if you've got access to a top-of-the-range soft-top Merc or Jag, with in-car fax and satellite TV, but I'm going to assume you are just an average spud like the rest of us. That means you are reduced to slapping on the shades and pretending you do actually have a dead-flash car but you've lent it to a mate for an hour or so.

*any resemblance to Major Clive Spondoolicks (retired) of The Maltings, 26 Horseferry Crescent, Guildford is purely coincidental.

Ingredient 2. The Wobbly

No self-respecting director would be without his ability to Throw A Right Wobbly. These temper tantrums are also absolutely vital for any self-respecting movie brat and should be dished out at any and every opportunity to all around you and over any incident, no matter how small.

Remember: the rest of Hollywood will judge you by the quality of your Wobbly. Practice on your younger brother (after all he's probably used to it).

WARNING! Use of the Wobbly should be restricted to when you actually are a famous film bod as throwing the Wobbly before then can result in getting lamped by some rough chaps.

Ingredient 3. The Personal Assistant

Personal assistants are vital to any young Hollywood honcho who wants to make it in TinselTown. Personal Assistants (PA's) are there to cater for your every need, whether that be lunch at Spago's or red jelly beans. However, as you are skint/unkown/smelly you will probably only be able to persuade a very thick person to be your PA. But at least you'll look like you have one and in this business, image is everything.

Your PA should be willing to slide down a cactus for you, to chuck themselves under a bus, to eat raw snakemeat if that is your hearts desire; in short, do anything you ask, whenever you ask . . .

Ingredient 4. The Name

Very few top-flight directors have ordinary names. Movie history remembers Eisenstein, Renoir, Orson Welles, Otto Preminger, Erich Von Stroheim, Francis Ford Coppola and more recently Quentin Tarantino. So unless your name is already Dirk von Mifthausen or summat, then you'll need to fish around for a fabbo director's name.

Step 1. The Idea

Right, you've got the specs, the PA and the moniker. What next? Well, the next thing you will need is **The Idea**.

Everyone in Hollywood has The Idea. Bus drivers have The Idea, petrol pump jockeys have The Idea, waitresses think about The Idea on their break.

The Idea is what your movie is going to be about. Is it a crime caper? A horror flick? A lovey-dovey romance? A cutting-edge new-wave musical black- comedy thriller with scifi undertones and a documentary sheen? Three men dressed as aliens rob a bank but accidentally choose an alien space craft as a getaway vehicle and end up in jail on Mars? A sensitive schoolboy sick of being bullied meets an old chinese man who teaches him old-style karate? Four mutant turtles living in a sewer learn kung fu from a rat and save the world?

Whatever your idea is it needs to be able to be summed up in about ten to fifteen words. So, a film like StarWars for example would be: 'Good guys in white, fight bad guys in black, in space.' Titanic would be: 'Big ship sinks. Almost everyone dies.' Get the idea?

Step 2. The Script

Once you have an idea (don't worry if you haven't got An Idea, just make a sequel, or rip off something that made boffo box office last year) then you will need A Script.

In Hollywood, big bucks are paid for film scripts with people making complete careers from the movies as writers, without ever having a film made! So writing is obviously quite a good thing to get into, knowworramean?

Anyway, once you've cobbled together some sort of script, and let's say it's called I Was a Teenage Tellytubby you can move on to . . .

Step 3. The Money

Now you've got the script you'll need to get Some Money to be able to make it. Getting money for your film is VERY DIFFICULT so you have several options:

a. Ask your Mum or Dad for a few quid, or an advance on your pocket money for, say, 500 years. Oh, and could you borrow the video camera?

b. Get a whole batch of friends to cough up, with the idea that when the film becomes a smash hit, they'll get shedloads of cash (canny Jack Nicholson asked for a share of the first Batman blockbuster when he played The Joker in 1989, raking in an estimated 50 MILLION DOLLARS!).

c. Sell your idea to a major Hollywood studio and get them to throw money at you. This is by far the best option but is by far the hardest, as, by the last count, there were 765,799,653,002 people trying to sell film ideas to Hollywood studios. For this option you'll need to move on to Step 4.

Step 4. The Pitch

This is the art of selling your idea very, very quickly. It will take you many years of trying to get in front of top Hollywood executives who decide if a film is going to be made. When you do, you can't waste time bumbling along. You have to have a short! sharp! snappy! 'pitch'.

For example, if you were describing a movie like Titanic, you would describe it as: 'When the world's biggest ship sinks, you are there!' and Jurassic Park might be pitched as 'Dinosaurs aren't extinct and they aren't happy'.

Work on getting the description of your movie down to about ten words or so. Then you can be certain of getting your pitch across whatever the circumstances are . . .

Step 5. Casting

Casting can be one of the trickiest jobs to get right. Hollywood history is littered with actors who famously didn't get film roles that shot others to stardom, or actors who were completely, totally, disastrously miscast. One of the most obvious is when actors play someone who is far too young; for example, Eric Idle played a twenty-one year old when he was fifty-six . . . Sean Connery played Dustin Hoffman's dad when Sean was just seven years older than Dusty . . .

Another common casting problem is when big stars get it into their heads that they want to play a particular role no matter how bad they'll be (eg: Brad Pitt playing an Irishman in The Devil's Own).

If your budget is a problem then you'll be casting unknown actors, or your mates and family in your movie. You'll need to 'audition' them to make sure they're right for the role, and to have really good laff at how rubbish they are.

Step 6. Shooting

This isn't, as it sounds, about guns but is what actually filming is called. Films aren't shot in the order of the scenes in the film, so you'll need to draw up a 'shooting schedule'. This is a list of all your scenes in the order you are going to film them and stops you wasting time setting up scenes, cameras and lighting only to have to do it all again later.

With all the scenes of your film being shot in a different order you'll need someone to do one of the most difficult jobs in the movies:continuity. This means someone whose job it is to make sure that all the details of a scene match. If an actor has some paint on his face in one scene he must have EXACTLY the same streak of paint on his face when it comes to the next take, even if that takes place six weeks later! There are many examples in the movies where the continuity has gone wrong; see if you can spot any the next time you watch a film . . .

You'll also need to know your dolly from your pan, your backlighting from your babyspot and your woofer from your tweeter. No, I haven't gone loopy, I'm talking about the technical terms used by technical bods like cameramen, lighting blokes and sound fellas (they can't ALL be men, surely?) to describe the types of effects they use.

When shooting starts you will need:
(a) A Very Big Mouth, or A Megaphone
This is to establish that you are the boss and everyone should do exactly what you do. This is actually the real reason that people make movies and is very good fun.

(b) Six Pairs of Hands

The downside to everyone listening to what you've got to say is that everyone will be asking you to do things, or tell them what to do. For example, Richard Attenborough had to direct 300,000 extras in crowd scenes when filming Ghandi! Unless you are the Hindu god Shiva then, like most of us, you only have the regulation issue one pair of hands and will have to fall back on hiding behind the camera to avoid the chaos.

You will, of course, have a number of Assistant Directors whose job it is to do anything you ask them to do. It's great! Assistant Directors are usually so grateful to be working on a real movie that they'll work for scraps and sleep in dog kennels. But remember! Although Assistant Directors are just for the movie and not for life you should never mistreat your Assistant Directors. Take pity on them from time to time and give them a bit of a pat on the head or let them look through the camera. It'll pay off in added loyalty and bring a real shine to their coats.

(c) The Skin of a Rhino

You'll need a very thick skin to withstand all the verbals you'll get from anyone who has any money riding on your flick and doesn't like what they see. In extreme cases, movie-studio bosses will sack directors and take over their film. The famous silent movie star, Charlie Chaplin, once 'kidnapped' his own film and took the reels across the state border to edit at a motel when his bosses wanted to get him off the movie!

(d) The Patience of a Saint

If you end up directing a movie with a big Hollywood star or two, you'll have to get used to dealing with the antics of those stars on set. With egos as big as Texas, stars can make your life complete murder.

Big stars have 'riders' as part of their contract to make the movie. The 'rider' is simply a list of all the things that the studio must provide to make the star comfortable (besides the 20 million dollars they are getting paid). These riders can often include the FREEEEKIEST pile of gubbins you can possibly imagine and it will be your job to explain to the actors just why you haven't been able to provide a twenty-four hour jelly bean inspector, or a golden drinking bowl for their pet ocelot.

Once shooting has finished then you are ready to move on to:

Step 7. Editing and Post-Production

Right, you've filmed your masterwork, I Was A Teenage Tellytubby, and, like all real directors you've actually shot enough film to make a three-hundred-and-twenty-seven-hour-long movie. You now have to cut that all down to a brisk two hours length in the editing room.

To help you in this process you'll need a large pair of sharp scissors, some sticky tape and a boy scout. The scissors are for cutting the various bits of film out. The tape is to stick the different bits of film together and the boy scout is to unravel the mess that the film ends up in (see diagram).

Once you have spliced the movie into some semblance of something that someone might actually want to watch, then you can move on to the next, vital step: flogging the movie to the punters . . .

Step 8. Marketing the Movie

Once it's all been made, the real business of actually getting bums on seats can begin. Modern movies often spend a lot on advertising and merchandise. The people who sold Jurassic Park actually spent more on advertising than the film cost to make!

And, since the film actually cost fifty gazillion dollars to make you can see that marketing and selling a film is taken VERY seriously indeed.

One of the first things that has to be done is to come up with the poster and 'tag line'.

A tag line is the clever line that ad people 'tag' on to a movie title to give customers some idea about the type of movie they're going to see. For example these are some of the most famous tag lines ever . . .

The space chiller Alien was sold under the line 'Alien. In space no one can hear you scream.'

For the sequel to the 1977 classic killer shark movie, Jaws, the tag line was: 'Jaws 2: Just when you thought it was safe to go back in the water.'

This was followed by our all time fave tag line from the schlock horror flick Blood Beach, a tale of creepy monsters who live under the sand at the beach. The tag for this was: 'Blood Beach: Just when you thought it was safe to go back in the water you can't even get across the beach'(!)

Get the idea?

Can you supply the tag line for our movie?

I Was a Teenage Tellytubby

\- - - - - - - - - - - - - - - -

Step 9. Feedback

Before a movie is ready to be seen by the great, spotty, unwashed masses (us), movie studios will often have preview test showings with selected punters invited to come along and tell them what they think. Little cards are given out and the audience has to rate the movie they are watching. Depending on the result the studio may decide to change bits of the film to get a better reaction. This is usually the reason that Hollywood movies always end up with a happy ending, no matter how ridiculous that might be. Movies must always leave the hero standing at the end. This is the Hollywood law. The only exceptions to this are when the hero has to sacrifice themselves to save the world, or the plane, or the boat, or the leading lady, or the dog . . . So be prepared to go back into that editing room and chop your masterpiece into shreds to suit the 'feedback'.

Step 10. Opening Weekend

This is it! Twelve years of pain, sweat, blood and tears has produced your baby, your pride and joy, Revenge of the Tellytubbies and you are going to actually seee if real live people are going to pay real money to see the movie. Nothing can be done now except to sit and wait. If your movie comes up against stiff compettition from, say some HUGE blockbuster type movie, it may die a pathetic death.

On the other hand, you must always remember that, despite all the research, all the planning, all the advertising, all the stars, the script, the casting, the editing and the feedback, in Hollywood, 'nobody knows anything'. What this means is that no matter how much Hollywood studios think they can predict what films will hit and which miss, they haven't actually got the slightest clue. Take Last Action Hero starring Arnold Schwarzenegger when he was at the absolute pinnacle of his popularity. A whizz-bang special effects action-comedy costing a zillion dollars, it couldn't miss. Except it did. It didn't make a bean.

On the other hand the tiny British movie The Full Monty, made for twelve pence and some jam butties, starring nobody really famous and with zero special effects went on to be the box-office smash of the year. Go figure.

UTTERLY NUTTY FILM FAX 1

They're all completely nutty, and they're ALL true!

In the credits at the end of every movie keep your eyes peeled for 'Directed by Alan Smithee'. Smithee has directed more movies than any other director. Why? Because 'Alan Smithee' is the name used by directors who DON'T want their own name on a duff movie!

Good movie characters don't die; they just get remade . . . Sherlock Holmes, the great detective, has appeared in over 211 movies! Other characters score highly as well: Dracula, 159 films, Frankenstein, 115, Tarzan, 98, Zorro, 71, Hopalong Cassidy (!), 66, The Durango Kid, 64 and Charlie Chan, 49.

The youngest ever Oscar winner was Shirley Temple, the sickeningly cute, ringleted muppet who made musicals during the 1930s and 40s. She got her prize at the grand old age of SIX! And this was after being in movies for two years! On the other hand, Jessica Tandy won her Best Supporting Actress Oscar in 1989 at the age of eighty!

In the original Star Wars movie, the evil Darth Vader, he of the black balaclava and wheezy voice, was played by FOUR separate actors! Body builder Dave Prowse was Darth's body, James Earl Jones was the voice, Sebastian Shaw his face (when it was revealed) and an unknown actor provided the heavy breathing . . .

OUCH! Struggling writer/director Robert Rodriguez was having trouble raising the money to make his 1993 movie El Mariachi so he took the unusual and extremely nutty step of selling his own blood!

The Oscars are the biggest movie event of the year and all the top stars attend, hoping to get one of the little gold statuettes. But did you know that the Oscars are called 'the Oscars' because a librarian at The Academy Of Motion Picture Arts, who present the Oscars, said that the little gold man reminded her of her slaphead Uncle Oscar!

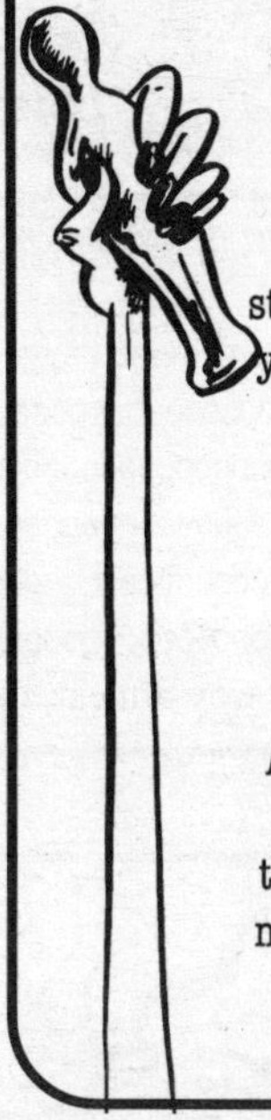

Movies often have crowd scenes using people who are called 'extras'. If a film needs big crowds then loads of extras are needed. The film that used the largest number of extras ever is the 1982 movie Ghandi. Director Dickie Attenborough needed a monster megaphone to control his 300,000 extras!

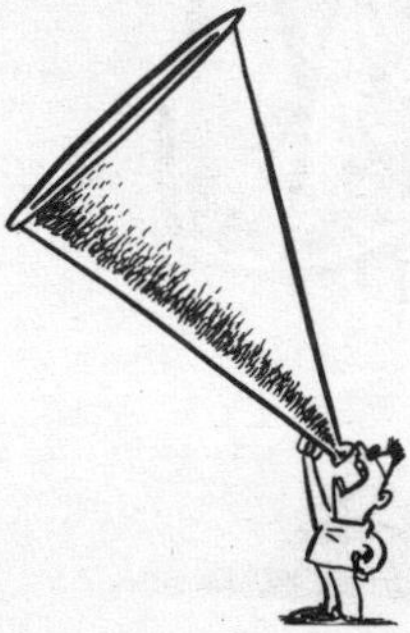

The legendary film director Alfred Hitchcock gave every film he made an unusual twist: he made very small appearances in every one of his many films. Often he would be simply walking past the main actors, or seen in a mirrored window, or reading a newspaper. A more recent Hollywood director, John Landis, has an even nuttier signature: he puts the line, 'See you next Wednesday!' in every movie he makes, including the famous Michael Jackson Thriller video!

JUST HOW BORING IS MAKING

Animated Films?

The simple answer is: animation is EXTREMELY boring. Let's show you why . . .

Animation is a very, very, very, very, very, very, very, very, very, very, sloow, very painstaking process, which is why almost all animators look like this:

Gazillions of drawings or movements are filmed, one by one, to build up just a few minutes of screen time. The way it works is that film runs through a camera at twenty-four frames per second. To make things appear to move, animators will draw around twelve frames per second with small differences from frame to frame. When the film is run, the drawings appear to move. If the animator is using models, like Wallace and Gromit, then those models have to be moved twelve times every second!

So, for one minute of screen time, an animator makes 720 movements. And that's if there's only ONE character! Each moving character or item has to be moved separately, so, if a film has five characters in each scene, all moving, then an animator must make 3,600 movements per minute! In a thirty minute feature this will add up to 10,8000 separate movements!

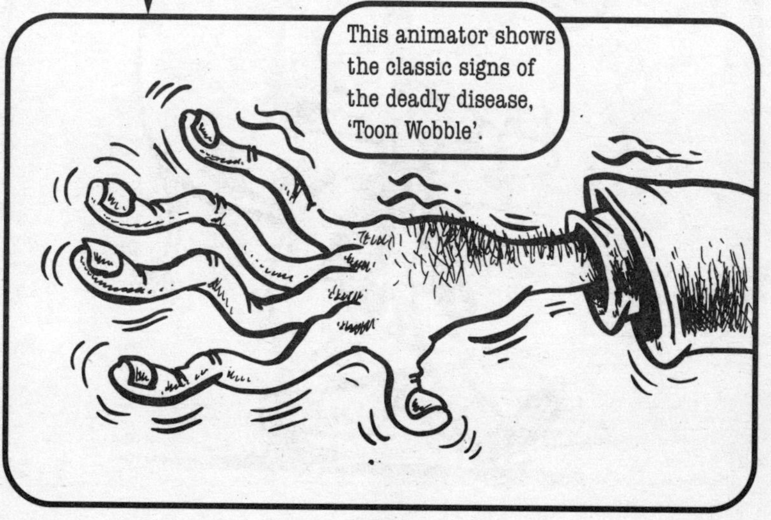

Of course if we look at something like a big Disney animation then we go into boredom hyperdrive. For instance, in The Lion King there is one scene involving a stampede of thousands of wildebeest meaning that each and every wildebeest had to be moved every second. This took a team of animators, who worked on this and nothing else, TWO YEARS to draw! I imagine that after two years of drawing wildebeest the animators were seeing wildebeest everywhere and needed counselling for wildebeest withdrawal symptoms.

This animator shows the classic effects that working in animation produces: the glazed, squinty eyes, the white hair, the wrinkles, the fat botty, the wasted legs and vacant expression . . . and this is actually Darren, a YTS trainee who's only been at the studio for three weeks. The effect that animation has on animators like Chip Scraggly (pictured below) who have been at it for over fifty years are too horrific to show before nine o'clock at night. So if you're looking at this before that time, STOP IT!

Another common problem for animators working for some time in the biz is that of 'Toonitis'. This is when animators begin to believe they actually are cartoons and, as such, completely indestructible! When a toon has a heavy object dropped on its head, a large comedy bump pops up.

However, this is not what actually happens when a heavy object is dropped on a real person's head.

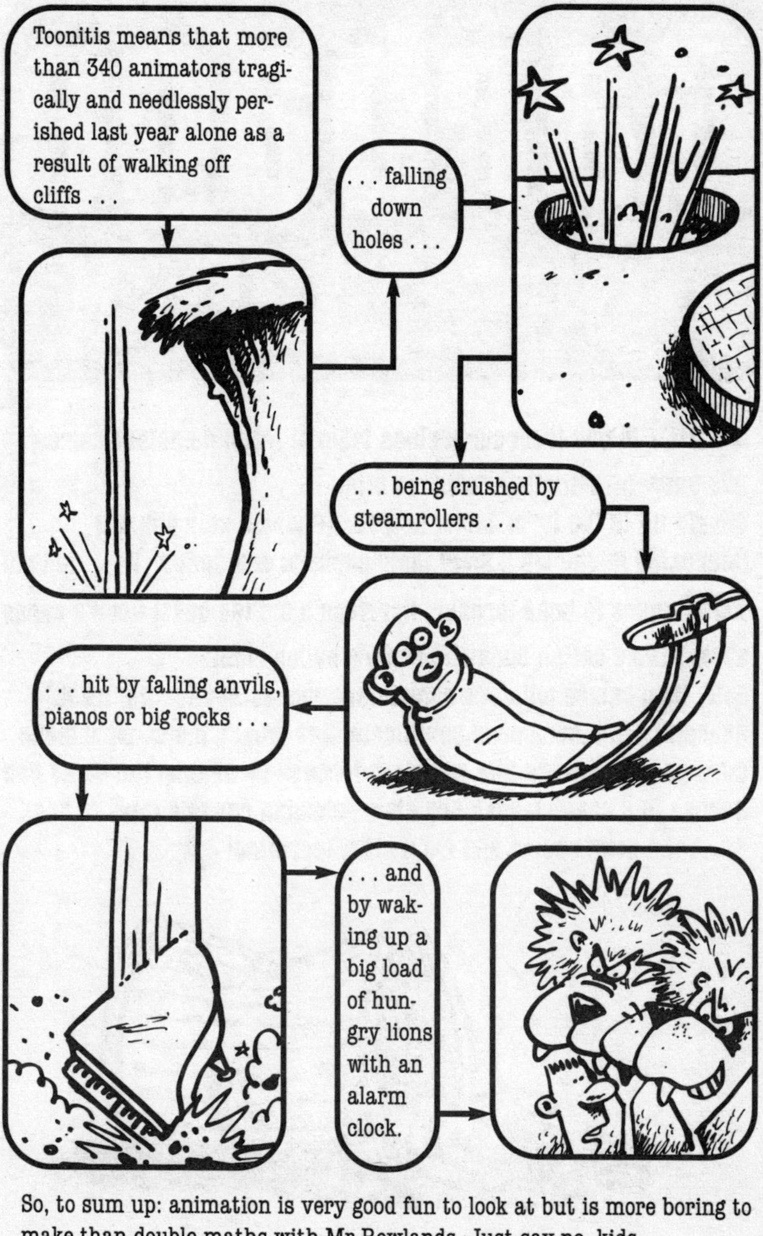

So, to sum up: animation is very good fun to look at but is more boring to make than double maths with Mr Rowlands. Just say no, kids.

Garbage of the Stars!!!

Direct to you from our trained team of trash detectors comes this once-in-a-lifetime fabulous offer.

Simply fill in the form below to indicate which star you are interested in and we'll steal their garbage and deliver it . . . to you!

Yes! Yours to keep forever: Harrison's old tea bags! Demi's nappy sacks! Leo's cotton buds and Arnie's bacon rind!

Each item comes with our completely non-authentic 'StarTrash' guarantee and numbered certificate. And what's more, we'll make sure you'll treasure this momento forever by sealing the items you choose in a custom-designed clear-viewing capsule (plastic bag).

So, make your choice and we'll start ferreting!

Just a few of the choice items we've dug up for our happy customers . . .

Slightly rotted fish head, Liv Tyler

Shreddies box, Matthew McConaughey

Ripped trainer, Richard Gere

Yoghurt pot, Claire Danes

YES! Rush me my guaranteed pile of TinselTown Trash NOW!

Julia Roberts Keanu Reeves Bruce Willis Woody Harrelson Demi Moore
Harrison Ford Will Smith Tommy Lee Jones Ewan McGregor Liam Neeson
Michael Keaton Piers Brosnan Sigourney Weaver Bugs Bunny Nic Cage
Al Pacino Robert De Niro Cameron Diaz Jim Carrey Arnold Schwarzenegger
Kate Winslet Winona Ryder Sharon Stone Sylvester Stallone Sean Connery
Laura Dern Jeff Goldblum Leonardo DiCaprio Mel Gibson Jack Nicholson
Danny DeVito Christian Slater Alec Baldwin Andy Garcia Charlie Sheen

all said that if we attempted to steal their trash they would sue us to within an inch of our bank account, but their names look good on the ad.

Name ________________________________

Address ______________________________

____

Tel number____________________________

Oh No!
It's The Loony Oscar Speech!

What can I say? My performance in this marvellous, marvellous, wonderful movie would not have been possible without the help of the sweetest, fairest, loveliest director who towers above all other beings like a colossus among, er, people of limited stature, darling, darling, lovely Brian Phelps, my mentor, my rock, my boss. Thank you, Brian! You know, on the tawdry streets of The City of Angels there are a million dreams, a million hopes and a million desires and I am one of the lucky few able to reach for that shining golden rainbow, pull it from the shimmering heavens, clutch it tight to my heaving breast, and see it bear fruit like some fruit-bearing message from God, saying, 'Yes, Gwyneth! Yes, it is you I have chosen to make the multitudes happy! You who is the chosen one who will one day give so much pleasure to so many with your role as the downtrodden beggar with perfect teeth in Terminator 4! But my stunning success would not have been possible without the sacrifice my wonderful parents made to straighten my bicuspid molars and fix my nose. Their unrelenting struggle against overwhelming odds, unbelievable heartache, pain, misery and human degradation showed me, showed me . . . sob . . . sob . . . sniffle . . . a love of cosmic magnitude beside which all other love is but a pale shadow struggling to even look like a shadow at all . . . sob . . . wail . . . and my grandparents, oh my grandparents who worked their fingers to the bone on the Stock Exchange to give my parents a start in life, without which I, me, The One, would not have been here! Can you imagine? A world without me? Oh thank you . . . sob . . . sob . . . I love you all! And, and YOU love ME! You do, don't you?

Waaah-ha haa-haaaaaaa!

WAAAAAAAH!

If Getting Up in the Morning was

AN Alien MOVIE . . .

Scene: an eerie, dimly lit corridor stretches in front of the camera. Smoke, or steam, billows from unexplained grilles and hatches. Blue light seeps out under doors as the camera tracks along and down into another dark room. We hear rasping, unearthly breathing sounds and we focus on a gently moving heap of rubbish, filth and general ickiness. The heap stirs, and Ripley (Tracey Ripley, that is, of 8 Bucklingford Close, Winchester) opens her eyes and adjusts her vest. She drops to the floor and rolls across the floor, reaching for an absolutely massive, lethal-looking toothbrush.

(off camera) Mum: 'Tracey! Get out of bed, you lazy moo. It's time for school!'

Ripley narrows her eyes at the noise. She moves silently to the door and, dropping down on one knee, points the toothbrush out ahead of her and takes a quick look at the corridor. Spooky clunks and bangs come from the door at the end of the corridor from where a blue light appears. Ripley backs up against the wall and starts to move towards it. Her breathing gets quicker and more shallow.

Ripley (whispering): 'OK, Mother. Let's see what you've got.'

As she approaches the door we hear a sound effect of clunking footsteps and slithery sounds approaching from behind, getting nearer and nearer. Ripley takes quick, panicky looks behind her as . . .

A horrible screaming wail comes from the room in front of her and Ripley bursts through, toothbrush cocked, locked and loaded. In front of her, lit by the flourescent tube lights, is a disgusting, thrashing mass of blubbery slime and goo, screaming and slapping its contorted face in agony.

Ripley: 'How many times have I told you to get rid of that Old Spice aftershave, Dad? Now move it! We're running out of time!'

Starts to kick Dad out of the bathroom.

Dad: 'NOOOOOOO! Please, Trace! I can't go out there! I don't want to go! PLEEEEEAAAASE!!!!'

Ripley steps up to Dad and slaps him quickly, one, two.

Ripley: 'Pull yourself together, man! You HAVE to go. There's no one else who can do what we need you to do. No one! Besides, you're the headmaster.'

UTTERLY NUTTY FILM FAX 2

They're all completely nutty, and they're ALL true!

Fred Astaire was, by most peoples judgement, the greatest dancer the movies has ever seen. He was a top Hollywood star for more than forty years. However, when he first auditioned for the Hollywood studios he got this report: 'Can't act. Can't sing. Slightly bald. Can dance a little.'

In the utterly rubbish 1978 schlock horror movie, The Swarm, the producers used twenty-two MILLION bees and then insured their stars against bee stings. No insurance company would insure them against appearing in such tripe though . . .

Movies use lights all the time. In the early days of moviemaking, because film then was less sensitive, they needed more light. The most powerful light ever used was a 13949 amp arc light used in a movie called California in 1928. Its beam was so powerful that it could be seen ninety MILES away!

The next time you are at the cinema and have a bad seat, spare a thought for the people who were in the back row for the film Boots, shown in the Oval Amphitheatre, Columbus, Ohio. That audience was the biggest ever movie audience: there were 110,000 people there!

In a bid for added realism, director Michael Curtiz instructed extras to throw REAL SPEARS at Hollywood legend Errol Flynn. When Flynn found out, he chased Curtiz around the set!

In Mel Brooks 1976 spoof comedy Silent Movie, the entire movie is 'silent' with no voices . . . except one. The only word spoken is 'Non!' by famously silent Marcel Marceau the French MIME artist!

The very first custard pie in the movies was thrown at comic Fatty Arbuckle in the 1913 movie, A Noise From the Deep. However, the pie was actually a blackcurrant and cream tart ordered from the studio bakery. Fourteen years later, Laurel and Hardy staged the greatest-ever custard pie fight using over 3,000 custard pies, which by then were made of shaving foam!

FILM REVIEWS
By Top Nutters!
VINNIE JONES REVIEWS ARMAGEDDON.

There's two sorts of films. Films I like and films I don't like. I like Die Hard 1, 2 and 3, Lethal Weapon and Lock, Stock and Two Smoking Barrels. I don't like You've Got Mail or The Rugrats Movie.

If I don't like a film then I'm gonna give it some, right? I mean, if I waste two hours on some doofus flick I'm gonna be well put out. Well put out. And if I'm put out then someone's got to be held responsible for that. Cos I'm hard. Well 'ard. I am. Ask anyone. But don't ask me cos I don't like it, right?

However, if I like a film, you can bet it's gonna be one pukka movie. Armageddon is very much a Vinnie Jones piece of work. Loud. A bit flash. Full of explosions. In fact, Armageddon might be the hardest movie ever.

Bruce Willis, the second-hardest man on the planet after me, is a really hard oil-rig type geezer, dead rich, dead hard and completely pukka. Get this: he's a millionaire oil-rig geezer, but he still gets stuck in with all the other lads. Gets oil all over his clobber an' that. And when a massive rock is gonna stick the 'ead on planet Earth he is The Man who has The Plan. In a totally well 'ard way he lands on the rock in outer space and blows the darned* thing up. The only thing what got right up my 'ooter was that Bruce got blowed up too. I mean, what happens when they make Armageddon 2: This Time It's Curtains?

Anyway, it's a top movie. See it. Or see me.*

*Not Mr Jones' actual words.

The Nutty Hall of Hollywood Fame

Channel Nutty's Top Film Critic, Softly Weeping, chooses his very own personal favourites from moviedom's rich tapestry of stars and salutes some of the superstars of cinematic history . . .

No1. Macaroon Conker

The first truly massive child star of modern movieland, Macaroon shot to fame with his first Hollywood project; You've Been Maimed! an hilarious caper comedy. In Maimed! Macaroon plays Filthy Rich, the richest kid in the world who is hilariously left all alone in a palatial house which is burgled by two hapless lower-class types. Much to everyones's surprise, Filthy maims the two low-lifes with a vast array of household items. Ho, ho ho. For his role in this pile of pants Macaroon received a trillion dollars and a new bike.

His follow-up movies never quite acheived the dizzy heights set by Maimed! and by age eleven, Macaroon was washed up, reduced to soap commercials and appearing with Steve Gutenberg.

Advertisement

EARN BIG BUCKS
AS A HUMAN HOLLYWOOD FOOTSTOOL!!!!

Yes!!! Learn how Hollywood's hottest movie moguls incredible laziness and cruelty can get YOU leaping up TinselTown's career ladder! Busy Hollywood head honchos just don't know exactly *when* they'll need a footstool, which is where you come in as a highly paid, mobile human footstool. Our detailed manual lets you know all the facts you need to join this fast-growing career; correct bending techniques, back-strengthening exercises, heel-scuff prevention, knee-pad suppliers and many, many more tips for succesful footstooling. Written by Gutless Fop, a famed footstooling expert with ten years experience as one of L.A.'s most sought after pieces of human furniture, *Turn Heels on Your Back into Dollars in Your Pocket!* will be one of the best investments you'll ever make!!!

YES! Rush me a mint copy of Turn Heels on Your Back into Dollars in Your Pocket! ... NOW!

Name ______________________

Address ______________________

____

____

Telephone ______________________

ANIMALS in the Movies

Hi, folks, I'm your oily host, Oily Host, joining you for a fabulous evening of drivel and tripe to fill in a few more hours in your worthless and pointless lives . . . oh, what's the point of it all, eh?

In a Channel Nutty Special, we salute the animal stars of Hollywood. From the earliest days of movies our furry friends have played a big part up there on the silver screen (why 'silver'? I've never seen one that wasn't a sort of dirty cream colour . . .).

We know all about cutey-pie mice (Mousehunt), adorable doggies (Beethoven, K9, 101 Dalmatians . . .), lovely horsies (Black Beauty), marvellous moggies (The Aristocats, The Lion King) and totally lovable, er, killer whales (Free Willy). But there are a host of other, unsung heroes of animal cinema who we now turn the spotlight on. And remember friends, all the items you'll see tonight have been completely tested for the correct level of nuttiness by trained specialists. Don't try any of this at home!

What? Wrong show? Oh, OK. It's that animal thing then.

NO. 1 BUDGIES

The only animals ever to win an Oscar, Bill and Coo featured in the 1947 budgie blockbuster titled, with stunning accuracy, Bill and Coo which wowed cinemagoers everywhere that year. The movie featured a bird town called 'Chirpendale' and all the parts are played by budgies wearing HATS and TIES! (This is true, by the way, not summat we just made up. I mean could you make that up? Well we could but, honest, in 1947 for some totally nutty reason someone made a movie about budgies and, even more amazingly, people watched it.) The only other appearance of a budgie is probably in The Birdman of Alcatraz where a feathered filmstar played opposite Hollywood legend, Burt Lancaster.

NO. 2 BEES

From birds to bees. In the 1978 disaster, The Swarm Michael Caine took a fat pay cheque to appear with twenty-two million co-stars, all bees. But not just ordinary, lovable, honey-producing bumblybees, these were vicious, African KILLER BEES! Caine reckons that if he does four movies, one might be worth watching. This wasn't one of those. Amazingly, after the movie was released, although Caine went on to appear in some brilliant movies and rake in the dosh, none of his co-stars continued in the movies . . .

NO. 3 ORANG-UTANS

Clyde, the hairy star of Every Which Way But Loose (1978) and it's sequel Any Which Way You Can, completely wiped the floor with his co-star, the little-known Clint Eastwood. Although Clyde won all the applause in both movies it was Clint who went on to further box-office glory. He never forgot old Clyde though and the two can regularly be seen on the razzle in Hollywood's hottest night spots. Probably.

NO. 4 FISH

One movie above all others stands out when it comes to discussing superstars of the Hollywood fish community: 1986's A Fish Called Wanda. The only movie ever to feature a scaly heroine, apart from Splash! and The Little Mermaid, Wanda shot its star to real fame in this smash hit. Audiences everywhere cried during the famous Wanda death scene. Co-star Kevin Kline (who eats Wanda in the film) recalls that he still gets hate mail from distraught fish fanciers across the globe. Other notable film fish are the killer piranhas in Killer Fish (1978) and, er, that's it.

Apart, that is, from the biggest and most dangerous fish in the Hollywood Ocean: agents. Here's one closing a deal . . .

NO. 5 WILD-BOARS

1984 was a big year for the large group of Hollywood wild-boar actors waiting patiently for their time to come with the release of Razorback, a movie about an extremely nasty and horrible killer boar. Prior to Razorback, wild boars had been restricted to bit parts in Robin Hood and other medieval type movies. But Razorback wasn't the breakthrough that the 'hairy pigs' had been hoping for and they had to wait another TEN years until Disney's The Lion King shot Pumbar ('THEY CALL ME MR PIG!', becoming a catchphrase echoing around the world) to real superstardom.

UTTERLY NUTTY FILM FAX 3

They're all completely nutty, and they're **ALL** true!

Actor **Robert De Niro** is famous for his method acting, which means that he really tries to be like the character he's playing, not just on the film set, but off it as well. In 1980 he took this to extremes when he played boxer Jake La Motta in Raging Bull. He not only learnt how to box, he ate until he had gained more than twenty kilos!

Clark Gable was one of the biggest movie heartthrobs of all time and was the biggest movie star in the world in his heyday. But he should be remembered for one nutty thing above all else: animator Bob Clampett (who invented Bugs Bunny) said that he got the idea after seeing Clark Gable eating a carrot!

Perhaps that can only be topped by another of the movies' method actors, **Al Pacino.** The American mumbler once had his TEETH FILED down to make him look older for his role in The Godfather 3! The gnashers were capped immediately after the movie finished . . .

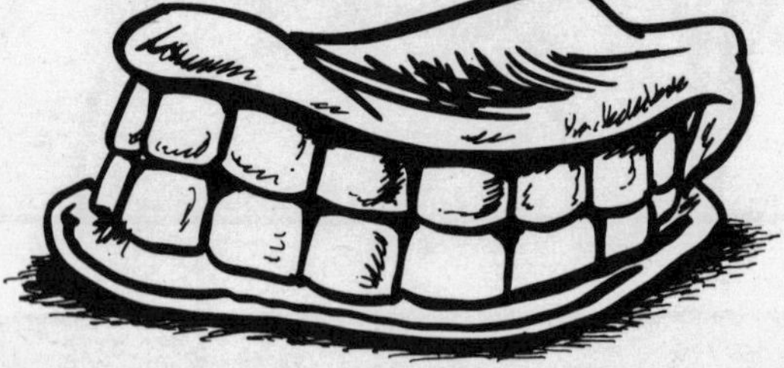

William Castle, a director who made schlocky B-movies in the 1950s was the king of gimmicks. Audiences for his films were treated to 'Percepto', which was a process that gave punters an ELECTRIC shock! He also hoisted four-metre long skeletons out over the cinema audience, invented 'Illusion-O' which consisted of glasses that allowed cinemagoers to see 'invisible' ghosts, and 'fright breaks' during the movie to allow nervous customers to calm down!

Another gimmick, not one of Castle's, was 'Smell-O-Vision', which pumped smells out into the cinema!

Fifties movie glamourpuss **Jayne Mansfield** loved all things pink. So much so that she had a pink house, a pink car, pink clothes and occasionally pink hair. She even dyed her pet poodle pink!

The Man Who Couldn't Smile. Buster Keaton, who was a big silent movie comedy star, was famous for his miserable mug at all times in his movies. Audiences liked it so much that they nicknamed him 'Old Stoneface' and his studio, MGM, had it written into his contract that he was never allowed to smile! The only time he did on camera was at the end of the 1927 Steamboat Bill Jr and after audiences saw it they objected so much that the offending smile was cut out!

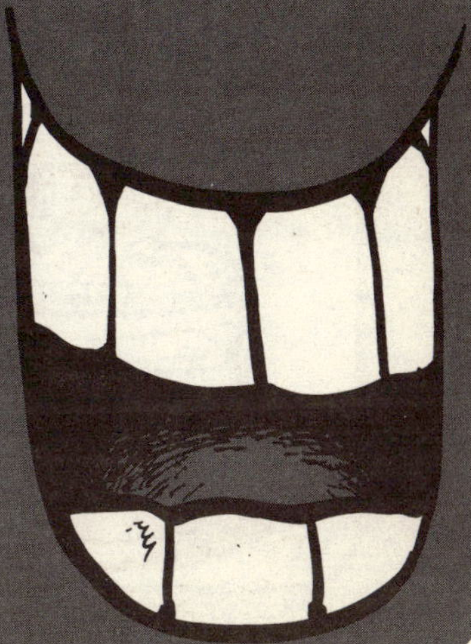

THE Nuttiest Movie Titles EVER!

In our guide to making movies we showed you that actually getting a movie up there on the silver screen was harder than, to pluck an example from the air, pulling twenty-four Luciano Pavarottis up a treacle-covered cliff during a snow storm by a rope tied to your ears, with your mouth full of porcupine quills.

Even the rubbishest, worstest, pantsiest, suckiest movie takes at least a year of somebody's life. So why would anyone spend any time and effort making this collection of completely nutty movies?

Fried Green Tomatoes at the Whistle Stop Cafe
Who Created the Yo-Yo? Who Created the Moon Buggy?
A Gnome Named Gnorm
I Am the Cheese
I AM A CAMERA

I Loved You Wednesday

I See ICE

I Was a Male War Bride

How To Stuff a Wild Bikini

Fat Guy Goes Nutzoid

Don't Worry We'll Think of a Title

M

The Cars That Ate Paris

The Egg and I

RoGoPaG

Why Do I Believe You When You Say You Love Me When I Know You've Been a Liar All Your Life?

Life Is Cheap But Toilet Paper Is Expensive

What's Eating Gilbert Grape?

The Perils of Gwendoline in the Land of the Yik-Yak

Ha, Ha, Hee, Hee, Hoo, Hoo

The Film That Rises to the Surface of Clarified Butter

Betta, Betta in the Wall, Who's the Fattest Fish of All?

All these titles are good for a giggle and it can be fun trying to find your own personal favourite bad titles. Here at Channel Nutty there is one movie above all others that we feel is worth the title of 'Best Worst Movie Title Of All Time' and that's this 1993 movie . . .

Night of the Day of the Dawn of the Son of the Bride of the Revenge of the Terror of the Attack of the Evil, Mutant, Hellbound, Zombified, Flesh-Eating, Sub-Humanoid Living Dead – Part 4

The Nutty Hall of Hollywood Fame

Channel Nutty's Top Film Critic, Softly Weeping, chooses his very own personal favourites from moviedom's rich tapestry of stars and salutes some of the superstars of cinematic history . . .

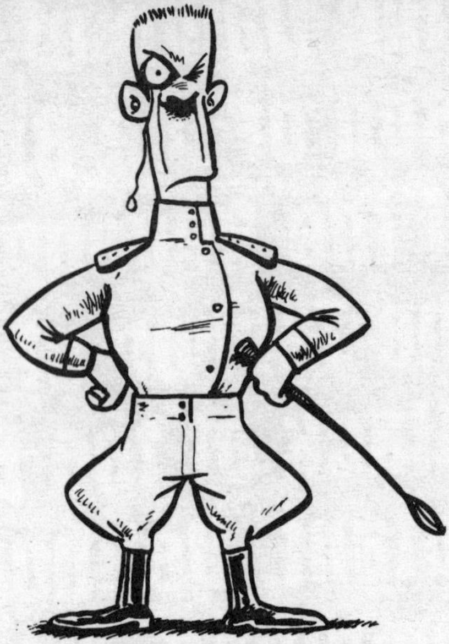

No.2 Erich von Schannibal

Von Schannibal was Hollywood's most feared director during the 1930s. Stars, crew, studio heads and writers all cowered in his one-eyed glare or were crushed under his shiny jackbooted heel. Known as 'Schannibal the Cannibal' after his habit of snacking on timid sreenwriters. He had been kown to eat as many as eleven of these harmless creatures at a single sitting! He directed more than 850 films in a career that lasted only ten years, until talking pictures arrived. With typical arrogance, Schannibal refused to believe that sound would catch on and made a forty-two hour silent, which cost the studio millions. He never directed again but did go on to stardom as an actor, making his final appearance in the 1974 turkey The Towering Poseidon Inferno playing himself.

From the director of Titanic and the producer of Independence Day comes the biggest film of all time . . .

GIGANTIZILLICA!!!!

On it's maiden voyage, the biggest passenger-carrying killer reptile ever made hits an iceberg! Only one man can save the movie.

Coming soon to a scream near you!
More terrifying than you can possibly imagine!!
Bigger than the most biggest thing you've ever seen!!!

STARRING: (in order of monetary value) Sylvester Stallone Mel Gibson Nic Cage Jeff Goldblum (he's in all these kind of movies, isn't he?) Jeff Bridges Bill Paxton and with special appearances from Jack Nicholson as Christian Slater and Tom Jones as Tommy Lee Jones.

Absolutely no girlies of any kind, this is an action pic and the only girlies trip over and twist their ankles running from the scary monster.

Written by Strobe Bullock. Edited by Vacuum Flaskton. Produced by Some Bloke. Directed by Bill Woo. A 1999 BigBuck Studio Production.

Harrison Ford Made My Bookshelf!

Movie stars weren't born movie stars, they all used to do other things before they earned millions and got themselves up there on the silver screen. For example, Harrison Ford (Air Force One, The Hunt For Red October, Star Wars . . .) made my bookcase when he was a carpenter! Well, OK, he didn't actually make my bookcase, but he was a carpenter. Here's a quick look at what some other past and present movie stars did in real life . . .

Geena Davis made a living as a costume dummy in a New York department-store window

Sharon Stone sold hotdogs

Sir Alec Guiness (the voice of Obi-Wan in Star Wars) wrote adverts

Sylvester Stallone had an exciting job: he cleaned lions' cages!

Pin-up Luke Perry made doorknobs

Michelle Pfeiffer worked as a supermarket checkout girl

Sean Connery was a male model, a professional footballer (almost) and a coffin polisher for a firm of undertakers

Jeremy Irons was a social worker

Sid James (the man with the gravelly chuckle in the Carry On films) was a diamond miner in South Africa

UTTERLY NUTTY FILM FAX 4

They're all completely nutty, and they're ALL true!

Film works by light being shone through the film running through a projector making the image much bigger on the screen. If you see a movie in a large cinema the image on screen will be around **500,000** times bigger than the film frame!

Awful, Blabby, Daffy, Dirty, Gabby, Gaspy, Gloomy, Hoppy, Hotsy, Hungry, Nifty, Shifty, Snoopy, Thrifty, Weepy and Woeful were some of the names rejected by Walt Disney for the seven dwarfs in Snow White and the Seven Dwarfs (1937)! Can you name the 'real' dwarfs?

All films need things called props, which are any object that the actors use or move around. These are usually things like glasses, chairs and so on. The biggest and most expensive prop ever was probably the £7,000,000 full-size pirate galleon built for the 1986 film, Pirates!

Talking of props, the 1939 blockbuster, Gone With the Wind, used 11,250,000 separate items!

Psssst! When Steven Spielberg, the famous American director was making Raiders of the Lost Ark in England he needed SIX THOUSAND snakes for a scene! The snakes made a big impact in the film but more than two thousand of them escaped and were never recovered . . .

Johnny Weissmuller, the most famous Tarzan, won FIVE olympic gold medals for swimming! His Tarzan was a big hit, mainly because of his musclebound bod. When he began to put weight on, the successful Tarzan series ended. Weissmuller's next bosses put him on a contract which made him pay five thousand dollars for every extra pound of weight he put on over 190!

The pavement on Hollywood Boulevard outside Grauman's Chinese Theatre, is famous for having the footprints and hand-prints of movie stars. The idea of getting stars to do this only came about after Sid Grauman saw the then mega-famous Norma Talmadge stepping into some wet concrete by accident in 1927. The comedian Jimmy 'The Schnozz' Durante, famous for his huge hooter, made his impression with that very same conk!

Nutty Movie Jobs

Fancy a job in movies but don't think you could cut it as the next Tom Cruise or Nicole Kidman?

Don't despair! The road to Hollywood takes many routes, according to a wise old man I once met in a Tibetan monastery. Or was that Brad Pitt? We can't all make it as stars, but we can all get jobs behind the scenes. Just take a quick run through Channel Nutty's completely unreliable guide to jobs in the movies . . .

1. Foley Artists

If you told your school careers teacher that when you grew up you wanted to fling half a kilo of strawberries at a length of chicken wire to imitate the noise made by a Klingon Death Crush, then they would probably think you were off your nut, mate, and send for the men in white coats straight away! But lots of people actually do make a living from matching up what you see on screen with the right noises. They are called Foley Artists. Why? Jack Foley was the chief sound man at Universal Studios, a true pioneer who once splashed a hose on to a bit of tin and, bingo! Instant Niagara Falls! Since that moment all Sound Effects people are called Foley Artists. They are constantly searching for EXACTLY the right sounds. Don't panic if you see a bloke dropping wet socks into a bucket of frogs. He's probably just a Foley Artist on the job! Or a nutter, it's your call.

2. Gaffer

The Gaffer is obviously a chap who looks exactly like your Grandad. Even if your Grandad doesn't wear over-alls, boots, a flat cap, a little tache and old shirts, he should. Gaffers are actually electricians. The reason they are called Gaffers is simple: nobody knows. Even more strange is why the Gaffer's Assistant is called the Best Boy or Best Girl (if they are a girl, obviously).

3. Boom Operator

When you're watching a movie, have you ever wondered what that small black thing is that keeps bobbing into the top of the picture? It's actually a microphone being operated by a Boom Operator. A Boom Operator is not someone who controls the explosions on movie sets.

A boom is a long stick with a microphone on the end of it. A Boom Operator is someone who operates that boom. His or her job is to make sure that the microphone just appears in shot from time to time so that know-it-all's with no life whatsoever can spot the mistake.

4. Make-up Artist

If you have ever seen movie stars in the flesh, then you'll know that they are nothing like the shiny super-beings who are up there on the silver screen. It's the job of the Make-up Artist to transform those plug-ugly thesps into the flawless creatures we know and love. It's a little-known fact that Leonardo di Caprio is, in actual fact, as ugly as a lobster, whose fizzog could stop the Titanic quicker than any iceberg.

Make-up Artists need heavy training on Army Assault Courses before they can handle life in Hollywood. The sheer amount of greasepaint, gunk and goo they have to trowel on means they need monster biceps and a grip of iron. So, get in training now for a career in the Make-up Department! And remember, your studio needs YOU!

A member of the crack Hollywood Make-Up Rangers springs into action.

5. Animal Wrangler

Free Willie, Beethoven, K9, 101 Dalmatians, Andre, Paulie are all movies that have one thing in common (besides being complete tripe, of course). That thing is: animals. Loads of movies star animals these days and, on set, somebody has to be in charge of them, teaching them their lines, getting them to the set on time, making sure they're comfortable and, most importantly, making sure they don't eat anyone famous.

Or poo on them.

'The main thing you have to have as an animal wrangler is patience. When I worked with Willy, the killer-whale star of Free Willy everything was fine. But, by the time we got around to Free Willy 2 things had changed. Willy was now a star and, boy, did he like everyone to know! I remember one time he refused to come out of his luxury trailer because he'd overheard a member of the crew refer to him as 'that big fish'. And then he began to live the high life: fast cars, big houses, art collections. When the bubble burst and the public got tired of killer-whale movies, Willy was left stranded. I think he's a chiropodist now . . .'

Hollywood Hit?

. . . OR MISS?

Take this quick Nutty test and find out if you could be the next Winona Ryder or Keanu Reeves!

Score high (mostly As) and we recommend you stuff your best knickers in a case and hightail it to TinselTown!!

Score low (mostly Bs or Cs), on the other hand, and you had better keep the day job, you talentless fops! There's only room for WINNER[illegible] La Land, LOSERS!!!

You are on holiday and the DJ holds a talent show. Do you:

(a) Leap on stage and wow 'em with your series of hilarious and uncannily accurate impressions?

(b) Slink behind the mike and mumble along to a karaoke machine?

(c) Leg it?

Your teeth, your gnashers, your toothypegs. Are they:

(a) A gleaming row of pearly white perfection?

(b) Not bad, but you can never chew silver foil again?

(c) Like a row of condemned houses, but more yellow and with icky bits of crud in between them?

Look in the mirror. Go on, do it.
Is what you see:
(a) So good looking it hurts, baby?
(b) About as exciting as a boiled spud and about the same shape?
(c) Hard to tell because the mirror seems to have broken?

Imagine that you have been offered a part, a small part, in a Hollywood movie on condition that you sell your dear sweet, twinkly eyed Granny. Do you:
(a) Flog the old biddy quicker than a very quick thing?
(b) Think about it carefully before seeing if you can just rent her out for a bit?
(c) What a dreadful idea. There's no way on earth that you would ever do anything so horrible!

Your mum has told you to clean up your room. Do you . . .
(a) Throw a complete, total, major wobbly, flounce off upstairs saying 'you want to be alone' then call security and have her thrown out?
(b) Grumble a bit and then go and do it?
(c) Mummy never tells you off because your room's always tidy?

Describe the way you dress.
(a) You're wearing a ravishing Galliano number with bias-cut lapels and hand-embroided gusset.
(b) Er, anything sloppy and comfy really.
(c) My mum buys all my clothes.

FILM REVIEWS

By Top Nutters!

KEVIN KEEGAN REVIEWS STAR WARS.

The thing that got me real excited about Star Wars, Episode 1 The Phantom Menace was the boy McEwan. He's an exciting prospect and no mistake and, by gum, he don't disappoint in this movie! He's m y sort of actor; always going forward, bit of a free spirit, loads of self-belief. All right, we know that he does end up getting topped by Alex Ferguso- I mean, Darth Vader in the later (earlier?) films, but who cares??? Movies are supposed to be about passion and flair and Obi-Wan's got that just right. The manager, Lucas, has put a big stopper right at the centre in Liam Neeson, recently transferred by local rival Steven Spielberg, playing Qui-Gon. And he needs it too playing at this level against the likes of Darth Maul, the top Dark Empire clogger, man-to-man marking right through; the sort of play that's spoiling movies all too often these days.

Now Obi-Wan and Qui-Gon nearly get caught in a sneaky offside trap in the Naboo swamplands but some fast footwork by a load of Kaadus, given a free role, spring them. My big problem though, Gary, is with Queen Amidala playing in red. And I hate red, I really do and if George Lucas wants to come up to St James Pa-,er, Craven Cotta-, er, Wembley, we'll see exactly what his evil empire's made of! Cos we're ready for him! We are! And this time it won't be pretty, I can promise him that!! I'm angry, I am!! Really angry!!! Sorry, Gary, he just gets right up my nose . . . I need to lie down for a bit . . .

The Nutty Hall of Hollywood Fame

Channel Nutty's Top Film Critic, Softly Weeping, chooses his very own personal favourites from moviedom's rich tapestry of stars and salutes some of the superstars of cinematic history . . .

No.3 Tamara Fluids

Tamara Fluids was the one of the biggest stars of the 1940s in Hollywood where she had an on-going feud with another popular star, Bette Cann. Tamara's heavily made-up fizzog dominated screens everywhere with her series of roles as perfect women. However, it was only after her death in 1972 that the world reeled with the news that Tamara was, in fact, not a woman at all! She was actually a pedigree, prize winning, long-haired border collie who, frustrated at her lack of success in breaking into Lassie movies, decided to pretend to be a woman and success soon followed.

MMMMMMMMM!!!!

If you're feeling peckish before the main feature, slip out to the foyer and grab one of our tasty new SNAK DOG COMBO'S! Yes! The Snak Dog Combo's not one, not two, but THREE tastee treat sensations in one DEEE-LICIOUS handy, stick-mounted chunk! Lipsmacking hot dog slurry on the outside!* Then, a layer of perfect pop corn whip! And, on the inside, the ideal end to any meal: a succulent ice-cream flavoured chemically-blended medley of flavours!*** You'll wonder why all food**** doesn't taste like this!**

*Contains only cow lips and ears

**Contains no pop. Or corn.

***Not actually ice cream, made with petroleum surface yield.

****Is not actually classed as 'food' by any recognized food agency.

SPORTING STARS

AND THE MOVIES . . .

If it's a quiet week at the cinema and there's nothing you fancy on, it's always a good laugh to see which pop star is currently making a fool of themselves by pretending to be an actor or actress.

David Bowie, Sting, Bob Dylan, Mick Jagger, Johnny Rotten, Diana Ross, Elvis Presley, Cliff Richard, Whitney Houston, Ice-T, Tupac Shakur (who was actually quite good), Cher, Jon Bon Jovi (you'll have to ask your parents or grandparents about some of this lot) are all pop stars who've made some toe-curling appearances in the movies.

CHANNEL NUTTY WARNING!

Unless approached with extreme caution, this is the effect that pop-star film performances can have on unsuspecting punters . . .

Amazingly, even Chris Rea, the completely ropey Geordie crooner was the leading man in a recent movie, which has been called 'the worst film ever made' by the Observer newspaper, who were so disturbed by how bad the film was they took three complete pages of the paper to warn the public . . .

More recently though, a more disturbing trend has come to our attention; namely sports stars getting in on the action.

If, twelve months ago you had said that Vinnie Jones, the ex-Wimbledon, Chelsea and Leeds midfield clogger, was about to become a leading man in a major Hollywood movie, you'd have been laughed at. Loudly. Yet, Vinnie is now set to appear opposite Nic Cage in a blockbuster movie called Gone In 60 Seconds (which was the usual length of time Vinnie took to get sent off) and is currently filming Gladiator with top director Ridley Scott (Bladerunner, Alien)!

Now, we're not saying that Vinnie won't make a good film star. We think he's ace. But we did a bit of checking up and found lots of other sports stars turning in ropey performances on the silver screen . . .

Michael Jordan, the US basketball player, made the cartoons he starred with appear three-dimensional in one of the most wooden performances ever seen in the cinema, in 1996's Space Jam.

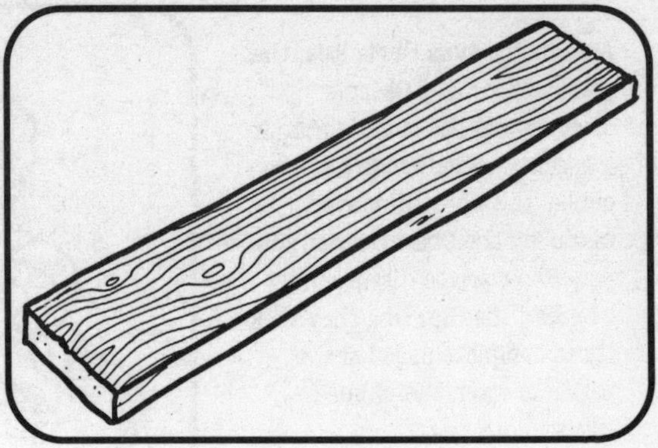

Fellow basketball star, Shaquille O'Neal, also made a film debut that year playing a very believable (not) genie in the 1996 movie, Kazaam!

Hulk Hogan, the US wrestling star, made a more convincing fist of his role as a reluctant nanny in the tripey Mr Nanny, perhaps because he had already had many years of 'acting' in the ring. Hulk has appeared in eighteen other flicks, with the high points being 1996's Santa With Muscles, 1998's 3 Ninjas: High Noon at Mega Mountain and 1999's Muppets From Space.

One of the all-time worst performances was that of one time tennis star, Vijay Amritraj, who appeared in Octopussy, a lame 1983 Bond film with Roger Moore. Vijay, a former Wimbledon finalist, actually played himself and, to make sure audiences knew who he was, carried a tennis racquet around at all times. This came in handy as a lethal weapon when Vijay was helping James Bond escape . . . He went on to 'star' in 1985's Nine Deaths of the Ninja, regarded by many as the worst-ever ninja movie: praise indeed considering how baaaaad all ninja movies actually are . . .

And who could ever forget the unbelievably dreadful Escape to Victory, the film in which the greatest footballer the world has ever seen, Pele, ends up in the same footy team as John Wark, the moustachioed ex-Ipswich player? With Sly Stallone in goal, Bobby Moore in midfield and Ossie Ardiles up front, how could the movie miss? Believe us, it could, easily.

So what have us moviegoers got to look forward to? Well, with Vinnie collaring all the bad-guy roles, look out for Michael Owen as the leading man of the next decade.

Also: Michael Schumacher as the next Bond villain and Tim Henman as Bond, Leicester City's Ian Marshall and Australian bowler Shane Warne battle it out to star in a remake of the 50s classic, The Blob. On a positive note, Liverpool keeper David James has been dropped from his role in the religious flick, The Cross.

Makes a change . . .

UTTERLY NUTTY FILM FAX 5

They're all completely nutty, and they're ALL true!

Although most of us think that Hollywood is where most films are made, it's not actually true. Around about 550 movies a year come from America whereas more than 800 films come out of 'Bollywood', the Indian Hollywood!

The biggest money making film of all time is 1977's Star Wars but when he came up with the idea, film-maker George Lucas had trouble raising any money. One studio said that no film with the word 'star' or 'wars' ever made any money. And the movie was nearly cancelled by 20th Century Fox, days before it was made when they got cold feet about it! The film ended up saving the studio.

The 1940s comedy duo Abbott and Costello, who were the biggest stars in the world, in 1942, once took out an insurance policy against anyone dying of laughter during one of their movies! Take it from us, that's a fairly safe insurance risk . . . (actually we really like Abbott and Costello, we only said that last bit for a cheap laff, sorry boys).

The credits at the end or beginning of movies can be really annoying when they go on a bit, can't they? In 1978 the movie, Superman had credits that lasted TWELVE minutes and those in the 1969 film Once Upon a Time in the West lasted for FOURTEEN minutes!

Wooooh! Spooky!
70s martial art chop socky maestro Bruce Lee died in mysterious circumstances at the young age of thirty-three. His son Brandon Lee went on to star in several movies and was on the verge of stardom when he too died at a young age: twenty-eight. He was shot dead when a gun used in the film The Crow was accidentally loaded with REAL bullets . . .

Imagine getting fired from your job before you were ONE year old! That's exactly what happened to several babies in the cast of the 1987 comedy Raising Arizona! The script required crawling babies and many of the babies learnt to walk during the production meaning that they couldn't be filmed and they got the boot. Boo hoo!

Did They Really Say That?

A Nutty collection of insults, foot-in-mouth moments and great Hollywood quotes . . .

She's like an apple turnover that got crushed in a grocery bag on a hot day

Camille Paglia talking about Drew Barrymore

If I die before my cat, I want my ashes put in his food so I can live on inside him

Drew Barrymore

I like children if they're properly cooked.

WC Fields

I've actually gone to the zoo and had monkeys shout at me from the cages, 'I'm in here when you're walking around like that?'

Robin Williams talking about his hairy bod

I'm a meathead. I can't help it, man. You've got smart people and you've got dumb people.

Keanu Reeves

Most of the time he sounds like he has a mouth full of wet toilet paper.

Rex Reed talking about Marlon Brando

My movies were the kind they show in prisons or aeroplanes because nobody can leave

Burt Reynolds

I am one of the most sensitive human beings on earth, and I know it.

Jean Claude Van Damme

Just standing around looking beautiful is so boring.

Michelle Pfeiffer

He has turned almost alarmingly blonde. He's gone past platinum, he must be plutonium: his hair is coordinated with his teeth.

Pauline Kael talking about Robert Redford

I have a love/hate relationship with Paul Verhoeven. He loves me and I hate him.

Sharon Stone

She's jumped right into the movie game . . . but I think people should learn to act first, you know what I mean?

Rosanna Arquette, talking about Madonna

People hate me because I'm a multifaceted, talented, wealthy, internationally famous genius.

Jerry Lewis

One of the most hostile, unpleasant guys I've ever seen . . . arrogant, sour, ceremonial, piously chauvinistic, egomaniac.

Elliott Gould talking about Jerry Lewis

OOOOPS!

Making movies is a tricky business what with all the sets, the actors, the technicians, the script, the general muddle and kerfuffle. It's no wonder that accidents happen. Accidents like these . . .

Uphill Rain

In the 1961 film, Mysterious Story, soldiers are escaping by hot-air balloon when they are caught in a heavy rain-shower. The problem: they are above the clouds . . .

The Case of the Disappearing Octopus

Master film-maker Steven Spielberg is prone to the odd clanger. In his 1985 movie The Goonies a character is asked what bit of the film was his favourite. 'The fight with the octopus', he replies. The only trouble was that the fight with the octopus had been cut from the final movie . . .

Loadsamoney?

The small-minded kidnappers in 1984's A Rare Breed demand two million lire as ransom. At the time that was worth about £350, not the £350,000 talked about in the movie . . .

With This Ring . . .

Fred McMurray played an umarried man in Double Indemnity in 1944 wearing a wedding ring throughout the film . . .

The Car With Six Wheels . . .

The all-time car-chasing movie, 1968's Bullitt had a scene with three hubcabs coming off Steve McQueen's car during a chase. When it crashes though, three more hubcaps pop off . . .

All Shook Up . . .

Elvis Presley, the king of rock and roll was rubbish as an actor, but that's got nothing to do with this story. In his 1957 movie he plays convict number 6239. You can tell because his number's printed big on his shirt. Later on though he's transformed into convict number 6240 . . .

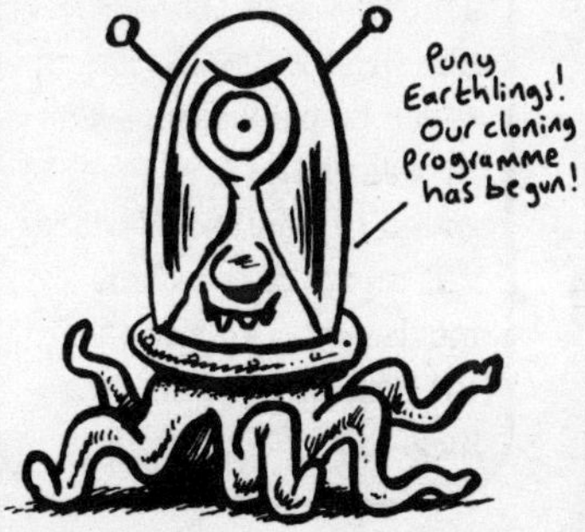

Doh!

The 1940 biopic Abe Lincoln in Illinois stars Raymond Massey as the great American president. In one scene he's waving to a crowd from the back of a train as it pulls out. 'Goodbye, Mr Lincoln!' shout various bods in the crowd.
Except one, who shouts, 'Goodbye, Mr Massey!'

UTTERLY NUTTY FILM FAX 6

They're all completely nutty, and they're ALL true!

Bugs Bunny, the wisecracking rabbit, is actually over sixty years old! He first made an appearance in the 1938 classic Porky's Hare Hunt. But he's a whippersnapper compared to his leading competitor, Mickey Mouse, who hurtled into stardom in the 1928 movie, Steamboat Willie.

In an effort to drum up some interest in their films, one early Hollywood promoter announced he would be giving away a baby on the movies opening night. Newspapers would take up the story and an outraged audience would pack the theatre to see the baby give away. The manager would give away a baby alright, a baby PIG!

Hollywood legend Paul Newman made his first appearance in a stinker of a movie called The Silver Chalice made in 1955. When, years later, the film was shown on American TV, Newman was so embarrassed by his performance that he took out full-page ads in national newspapers that said: 'Paul Newman apologizes every night this week'!

Prince Charles in Movie Shock!
Yes, HRH the Prince of Wales, appeared alongside John Cleese in the 1991 film Grimes Goes Green, in which he played himself. He wasn't the first royal to get on to celluloid; Edward VIII was in three silent movies, but Charles was the first to have his own lines . . .

The Secret Of Lassie's Limp. Lassie the collie starred in gazillions of ropey movies in the 1940s and then on TV in the 70s. In one movie Lassie had to limp, a difficult trick for a pooch. The secret was a blob of chewing gum wedged under Lassie's paw!

When Ed Wood Jnr (who has the honour of being The Worst Movie Director In History by a long way) was making his awful classic, Plan 9 From Outer Space he had Bela Lugosi, the Hollywood star of the 1930s as his star. Unfortunately Lugosi died only four days after filming started. Ed Wood didn't bat an eyelid and used a stand-in: his wife's dentist!

In the computer-animated Toy Story the animators perfected the movement of the plastic soldiers by glueing their feet to a wooden plank and trying to walk on them!

WOULD YOU CREDIT IT?

Movie credits, those things at the end (usually) of films that tell you who does what, are often well worth staying in your seat for. We've gathered some of the more unusual credits ever in Channel Nutty's guide to the nuttiest movie credits of all time . . .

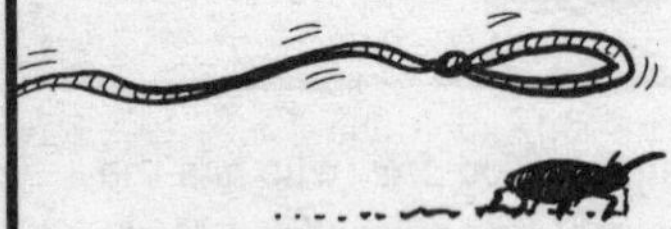

The 1959 horror movie, Creepshow had a credit for Cockroach Wrangler. The movie contained scenes involving THOUSANDS of live cockroaches!!!

1989's True Blood had a credit for the Wyoming Film Commission. Thing is, the movie is neither set or filmed in Wyoming. Go figure . . .

What do you think the 'Assistant Footsteps Editor' did in 1984's The Killing Fields?

Talk about starting at the bottom and working your way up: the 1978 movie The Greek Tycoon had a credit for the 'Assistant to the Assistant to the Second Unit Publicist'! The only way is up, I guess.

The credit for the story in the 1966 movie Lt Robinson Crusoe is to 'Retlaw Yensid'. Never heard of him? Try spelling it backwards . . .

The 1985 movie Special Effects has no special effects.

1947's Miranda was the tale of a mermaid, played by Glynis Johns. The credits included one for 'Tail by Dunlop'.

You'll be glad to know that the dog star of 1978's In Search Of Anna was fed, according to the credits, on . . . 'Loyal Dog Food'.

The credits for both the 1990 Spanish movie, Don Juan, My Dear Ghost and the 1969 Por Que Te Engana Tu Marido, which was also, fairly obviously, Spanish, were SUNG . . .

Horror-movie director, Philippe Mora obviously had too much time on his hands during the filming of his 1987 meisterwerk, The Marsupials:The Howling III which gave him a credit . . . for cooking eggs!

Check those shiny shoes out if you're ever watching Scent of Mystery (1961) where, for some completely loopy reason, there's a credit for the SHOE POLISH used on the shoes of the cast and crew . . .

The 1984 comedy, Night Patrol was set in America and was about a group of LA cops. It was an American movie, for American audiences with an American cast. The credits were all in French . . .

The 1954 movie, Her Twelve Men was about a kindly teacher, played by Greer Garson and her class of, er, thirteen . . .

OOPS! Chris Haywood got a big break when he appeared as the leading man in the 1987 movie The Bit Part. He wasn't so chuffed when he sat down to watch the film and realized that his name had been MISSPELT in the credits . . .

In 1989's The Bear, there are hardly any spoken words and only three human actors. Yet the credits list FOUR, count 'em, casting directors!

All mixed up . . .
Director Mike Snow made a 1969 film called ⟷
That's nutty enough, but he then went and plonked the credits in the MIDDLE of the movie!

Actors get very touchy about their credits. Golden-age Hollywood star Spencer Tracy thought that he deserved top billing above co-star Katherine Hepburn in the 1949 movie Adam's Rib.

His producer, scared of Hepburn's reaction, asked Tracy if he had heard of the saying 'ladies first'?

Tracy looked at him and spat: 'This is a movie, not a lifeboat.'

The most people ever to be credited on a movie is 743, for the 1989 movie Who Framed Roger Rabbit?

The 1968 disaster flick, Krakatoa East of Java about the real-life volcano was a box-office hit. The only problem was that Krakatoa is actually 200 miles WEST of Java . . .

The 1970 movie about a Korean War filed hospital, M*A*S*H had it's credits read out over a speaker system while the film rolled . . .

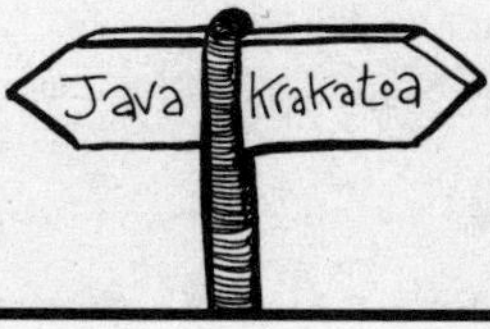

The End.
That's It!
There Is No
More!!!
Go On,
Clear Off!

CREDITS

Based on the novel Just Plain Nutty by Martin Chatterton from an idea by Martin Chatterton with additional material stolen from anywhere we can get our hands on it really

Original Screenplay Martin Chatterton

CAST

Martin Chatterton	Himself
Channel Nutty Presenter	Martin Chatterton
Ancient Geezer	Martin Chatterton
Bloke in Background	Martin Chatterton
Woman in Fishshop	Martin Chatterton
Young Martin Chatterton	Danny Chatterton
Bingo Caller	Martin Chatterton
Lighting	60-watt daylight bulb
Location Manager	Ann Chatterton
Mr Chatterton's Assistant	Sophie Chatterton
Mr Chatterton's Hair	Hair Apparent, Southport
Mr Chatterton's Wardrobe	MFI
Location Catering	The Lal Qila
Gaffer	Martin Chatterton
Best Boy	Me, of course
Best Girl	Leah Thaxton
Better Girl	Pippa Durn
Animal Wrangler	Martin Chatterton
Spiritual Advisor to Mr Chatterton	Homer Simpson
Doughnuts	The Dutch Bakery, Southport
Editor	Richard Scrivener
Producer	Martin Chatterton
Director	Martin Chatterton

If you enjoyed this book, why not try some more nuttiness?

The Utterly Nutty World of the Future

The Utterly Nutty History of Footy

The Utterly Nutty World of Sport

The Utterly Nutty World of Animals